26 Wishes

Written and illustrated by Renee Hazen

HAPPY
2ND Birthday
LIAM!

The day you were born into this world you were brought,

I looked into your
eyes and I sat and I
thought.
Your whole life in front
of you, how full it will be.
Here's 26 wishes
to you from me.

A is for art
beauty alive in activity.
may your life be full of
color and creativity.

B is for belly laugh
that makes you
shimmy and shake,
laughter so hard
it makes your cheeks
ache.

C is for courage
to face your fears,
to stand in pure light
and wipe away tears.

D is for dance
move to the rhythm and
beat. Life has a song
so move your feet.

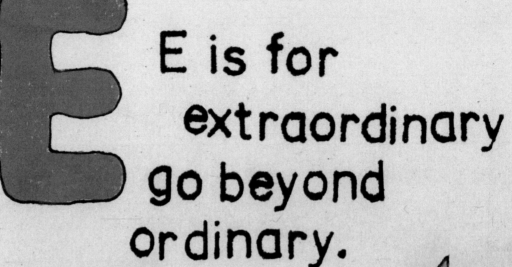

E is for
extraordinary
go beyond
ordinary.

F is for friendship
loyal and true,
whether it's Mr. Bunnyman
or somebody new.

G is for generosity
give graciously to all.
Acts of kindness are
needed no matter
how small.

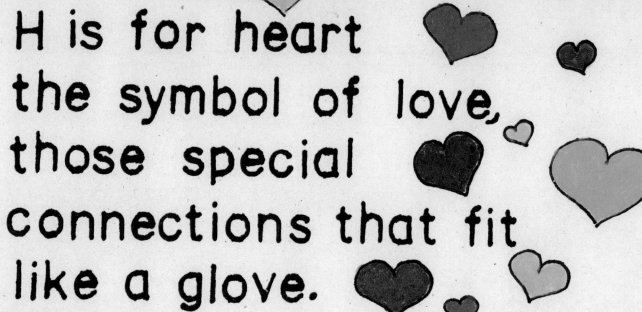

H is for heart
the symbol of love,
those special
connections that fit
like a glove.

I is for imagination
believe in the crazy,
like a polk a dot robot
with the head of a
daisy.

J is for jump
take a leap of faith,
whether it's your first jump
or your hundred and eighth.

K is for kinship
keep your friends and family
close. In good times and bad
they love you the most.

L is for luminous
a glow from within,
may your inner beauty shine
like a glow bugs rear end.

M is for magic
wondrous happenings
to be had,
your life will have many
spectacular and rad.

N is for nice
be friendly and sweet,
lend a hand pitch in
help those that you meet.

O is for oak
mighty and strong,
may you be brave
as life goes along.

P is for poetry
words in motion,
mystery and beauty
like the waves in the ocean.

Q is for quiet
in the darkness of night,
where dreams become
real and a hippo takes
flight.

R is for rocket
the sky is the limit,
life without fences
live in the minute.

S is for song
the rhythm the chorus,
the melody is a bird
flying free in the forest.

T is for tuft of grass between your toes, take time for the small things like smelling the rose.

U is for unique
like a snowflake in winter,
what makes you special
is your sparkle and glitter.

V is for voice
self expression through
sound, may the words
that you need always
be found.

W is for wisdom
like the owl in a tree,
to be truly happy
knowledge is key.

X is for exclamation mark
punctuate your life.

Y is for yowl
shout howl and gleam,
when you live life out loud
you will radiate and beam.

Z

Z is for zany
be silly and fun,
when you count up your
regrets make sure you have
none.

Made in the USA
Columbia, SC
11 November 2018